Bradley T. Morris

“I dedicate this story to my mom who was always cleaning up after me as a kid. Thank you for teaching me that a clean home makes for a happier mind.”

Sauryn Majik

“I dedicate this story to everyone on the whole Earth.”

Consuelo Gundermann

“My hope is that this story inspires your inner strength to stay true to yourself.”

ISBN: 978-1-7778939-7-2 (Paperback)
ISBN: 978-1-7778939-6-5 (Hardcover)

Written By: Bradley T. Morris & Sauryn Majik
Illustrated By: Consuelo Gundermann
Book Design By: Céline Sawchuk
Edited By: Amy De Nat

Printed by IngramSpark, Inc., in the United States of America.
First printing edition 2021
IngramSpark 14 Ingram Blvd, La Vergne, TN 37086, United States

www.MajikKids.com

majikkids presents

THE MESSIEST DAY OF MY ENTIRE LIFE

Some days are good, some are great, some are hard, some are bad, some seem to drag on forever, while others whiz by at the speed of light... and some days are just plain messy. This story is about the messiest day of my entire life. I hope it makes you feel better about whatever kind of day you're having!

So, it all began on an ordinary day.
A day just like most other days.

I woke up,
I went to the bathroom,
I brushed my teeth,
and then it started.

O's

I drooled all over my pyjamas.
Not a big deal, you know.
I just put on a new shirt.
I walked downstairs and had
a bowl of cereal for breakfast.
When my dad came downstairs and said,

"GOOD MORNING,"

I turned to say good morning back,
but my elbow bumped my bowl of cereal,
spilling it all over the floor.

Again, not a big deal. The dog ate most of it, and I mopped up the rest and then continued with my day.

But then, when my mom came into the kitchen, as she made her cup of coffee, the coffee press slipped out of her hands and shattered all over. And now there was coffee and glass all over the kitchen floor that we had to clean up.

Things were messy. While my parents cleaned up all the glass and coffee in the kitchen, I decided to go outside and get some fresh air.

As soon as I got outside, I noticed a big puddle right at the bottom of my steps. And so, I jumped from the very top step all the way down into the puddle and...

SPLASH!

It was no shallow puddle. The mud sprayed up over my head and our house and splattered all the windows and covered the car. My dad had to come out and hose off everything. While he did that, I walked back inside to paint.

But while I painted a picture of the muddiest day ever, my dog's tail knocked over my paint set, and the paint fell on the floor and splattered everywhere—

on the walls, on the floor, and on my dog.

My dog looked like a furry rainbow.

After we cleaned up the paint and gave the dog a bath, it was almost time for lunch, and I was kind of hungry. So, Mom made me some spaghetti. While I sat at the table, eating my spaghetti, everything was going just fine.

But then a big sneeze snuck up on me.
My head jerked back and shot forward.
Before I knew what happened,
my chin hit my bowl, and my bowl flipped
way up in the air and landed on my head.
My hair was red from the sauce.
I had noodles everywhere, including
in my ears and up my nose.

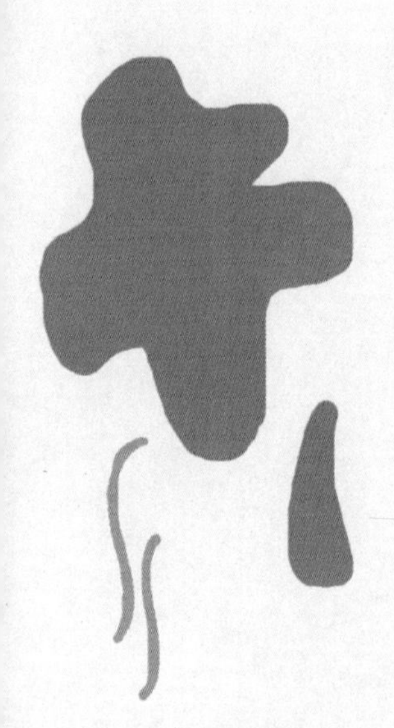

My hair was stained red the rest of the day.

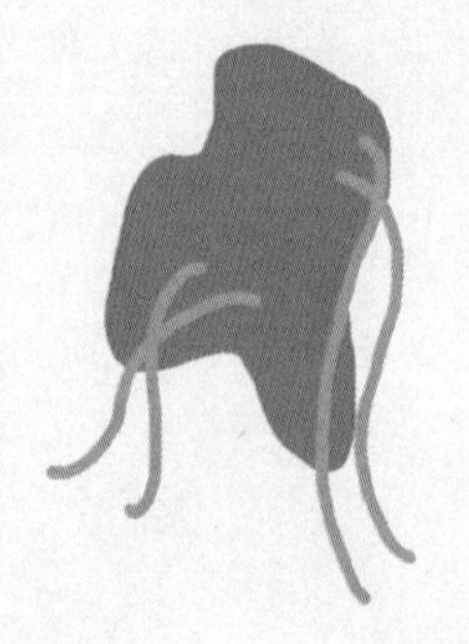

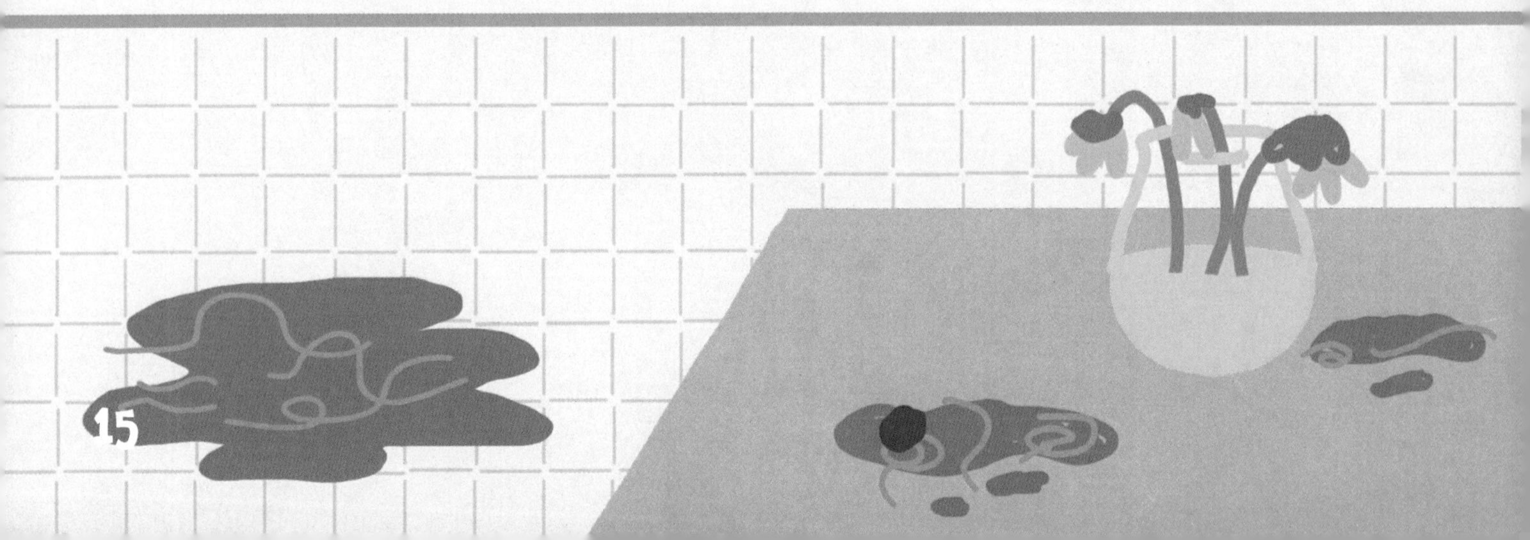

After the lunch debacle, I had to get away from the house. Everything was such a mess! And so, we decided to walk the dog at the dog park.

When we got to the dog park, I slipped on some wet grass and got grass stains all over my brand-new white pants. I was pretty upset, but my mom said not to worry because she could get the green stains out.

As we walked, my dog chased something into the forest and that something turned out to be a skunk. Oh, great, the skunk sprayed him, and man, did he stink!

When I tried to run away from my stinky dog, I stepped in dog poop, slipped, and landed on my back in a mud puddle with my smelly dog standing over me and licked my face. Everything around me was stinky!

After we left the dog park, we went to my friend Rumi's farm and fed his pigs some celery sticks. I guess I leaned over the fence a little too far because...

I flipped over it and fell into the pig muck right on my head.
I don't know if you know this about pig muck, but it's pretty stinky.
And I sure stunk— almost as bad as my stinky old dog.

So, my mom took me down to Rumi's pond and threw me into the water to clean me off. Except it was the end of summer, and there was no more water in the pond. I landed, splat, right in a deep, dark pond of mud. Not only was I pig-mucky, but I was also mud-muddy.

SPLAT!!

SSI-21

I couldn't even get in our car to drive home. Rumi's dad, the farmer, had to put me in the back of his truck with the hay bales and chickens to get me home. When I got back, and I got out of the truck, hay from the bales and feathers from the chickens stuck to my body, covering me. I looked like a big feathery chicken monster. Oh, man! It took a long time for my dad to hose me off to get me clean again.

P

Dry and dressed, I went inside and dad had made us some French fries for dinner. When I squeezed some ketchup on my plate, the ketchup bottle wouldn't stop squirting ketchup.

Plbbbbbtttt.

Ketchup squirted all over me—all over my mom, my dad, my dog, the walls, the windows, the floor, and the ceiling. There was ketchup everywhere! We eventually got that mess cleaned up, and it was time for dessert. I had a little chocolate ice cream while listening to my favourite song.

The music made me want to dance, and so I set my chocolate ice cream down on the couch and danced. But, when I sat back down on the couch, I forgot my chocolate ice cream was there and...

SPLAT!

I sat in my bowl of ice cream, smearing a big, brown, chocolate stain. Oh, man, this was the fourth pair of pants today!

What a messy day it was! Well, I'd had enough. I went upstairs to have a bath and brushed my teeth in the tub so that I wouldn't drool on my pajamas again. Clean and dry, I crawled into bed.

And so I had to sleep. And just as I was falling asleep, a fly landed on my nose and tickled it so much that...

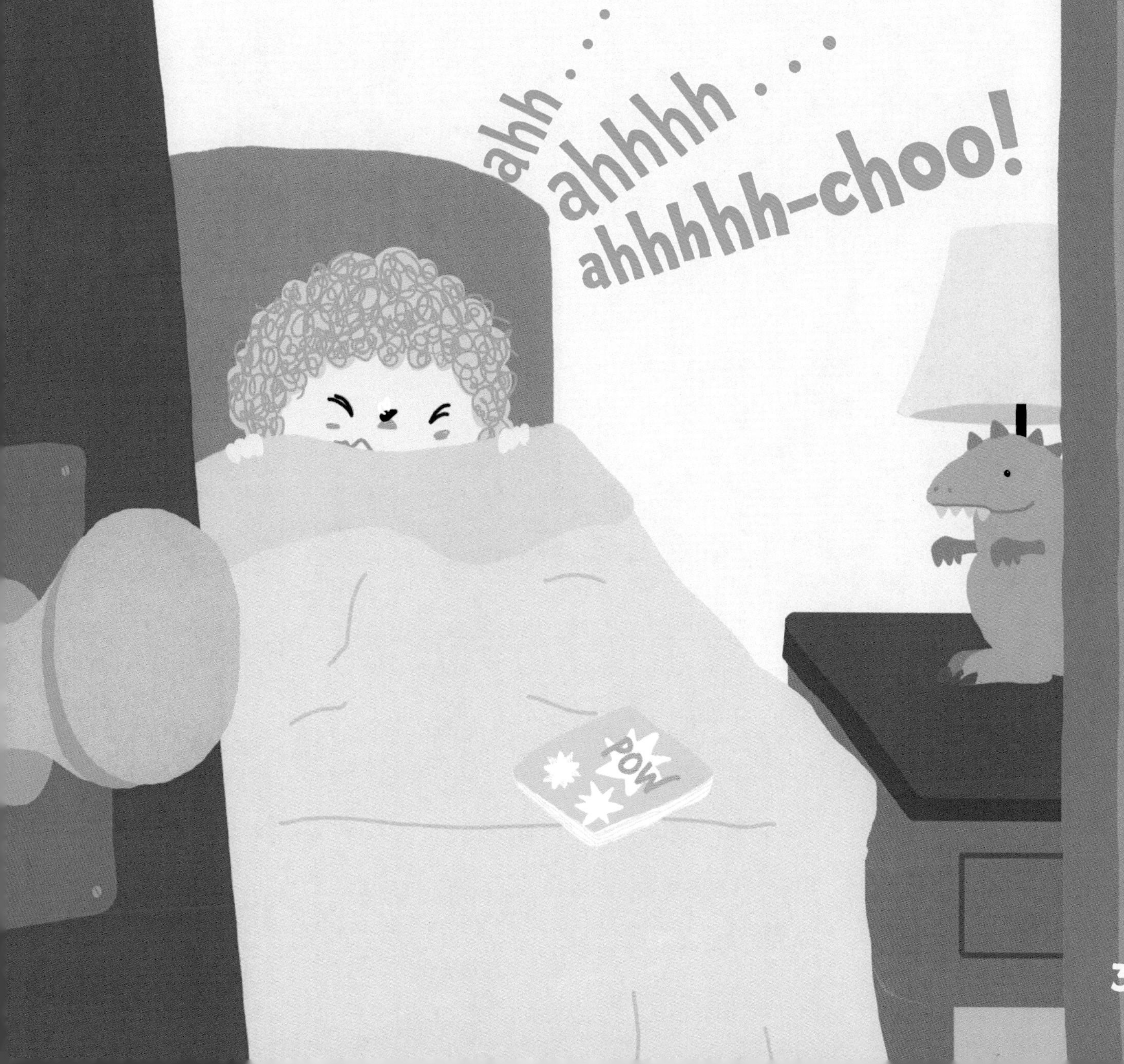

ahh . . .
ahhhh . . .
ahhhhh-choo!

I sneezed so loud and so big that boogers shot all over my sheets, all over my walls, all over my pyjamas, and all over my entire bedroom! We had to bring in our garden hose to clean my room, and then I had to sleep with Mom and Dad in their bed.

AND THAT WAS
THE **MESSIEST** DAY
OF MY ENTIRE LIFE.

Join the majikkids club

fun for the whole family!

Be the first to hear our new stories & meditations, access our downloadable colouring books, get games, activities, cool conversation starters, discounts on books and other magical stuff that's fun for the whole family! Enjoy a sample of what's included in the Majik Kids Club in the following pages...

www.MajikKids.com/Club

Colour the Book

Get the full activity book & colouring book when you join the Majik Kids Club!

Conversation Starters

Either answer the questions in writing inside the lined area OR better yet, share your answers with a friend, at the dinner table with your family or with your classmates. This is a fun way to get to know the people you love spending time with.

When was the messiest day of your life and what happened?

Do you feel calmer when your space is messy or when it's clean?

What's your favourite way to get messy?

Bold, beautiful and messy you!

Draw a picture of your messiest day ever.

Describe it to a family member, friend or class.

To listen to an audio version of this story and to find many more magical books, join the Majik Kids Club at

www.MajikKids.com/Club!

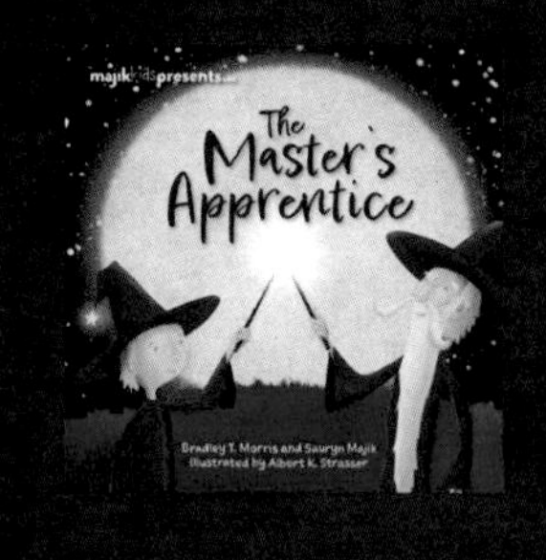

Bradley T. Morris is the creator of Majik Kids, founder of Majik Media. He loves writing stories, making cool media and waking people up to remembering that life is truly awesome and magical. His passion-hobby is playing pro golf.

Sauryn Majik is the co-founder of Majik Kids. He's also five years old. He also loves making up stories, laughing, playing and using his imagination to create worlds. He also thinks adults need to have more fun and lighten up a bit.

Consuelo Gundermann is a graphic designer who found her passion in illustrating children's books. She loves creating silly characters and the magic worlds they live in. When she is not drawing, Consuelo goes hiking in the woods where she can share her passion for Nature with her daughter Clara.